POOL PROBLEM

by Diana G. Gallagher

illustrated by Brann Garvey

Claudia Cristina Cortez is published by Stone Arch Books
151 Good Counsel Drive, P.O. Box 669
Mankato, Minnesota 56002
www.stonearchbooks.com

Library of Congress Cataloging-in-Publication Data
Gallagher, Diana G.
    Pool problem / by Diana G. Gallagher ; illustrated by Brann Garvey.
        p. cm. — (Claudia Cristina Cortez)
    ISBN 978-1-4342-1577-2 (library binding)
    ISBN 978-1-4342-1758-5 (paperback)
    [1. Swimming pools—Fiction. 2. Decision making—Fiction. 3. Hispanic
Americans—Fiction.] I. Garvey, Brann, ill. II. Title.
    PZ7.G13543Po 2010
    [Fic]—dc22
                                        2009002548

Summary: Claudia is super excited because her family is getting a pool! But her
tree house tree needs to be cut down to make room for the new pool. Claudia has
so many happy memories in the tree house. How can she leave it behind? Stuck
between the past and a pool, what's a girl to do?

Creative Director: Heather Kindseth
Graphic Designer: Carla Zetina-Yglesias

Photo Credits
Delaney Photography, cover

Table of Contents

Cast of

ME

CLAUDIA

That's me. I'm thirteen, and I'm in the seventh grade at Pine Tree Middle School. I live with my mom, my dad, and my brother, Jimmy. I have one cat, Ping-Ping. I like music, baseball, and hanging out with my friends.

MONICA

MONICA is my very best friend. We met when we were really little, and we've been best friends ever since. I don't know what I'd do without her! Monica loves horses. In fact, when she grows up, she wants to be an Olympic rider!

BECCA

BECCA is one of my closest friends. She lives next door to Monica. Becca is really, really smart. She gets good grades. She's also really good at art.

ADAM

ADAM and I met when we were in third grade. Now that we're teenagers, we don't spend as much time together as we did when we were kids, but he's always there for me when I need him. (Plus, he's the only person who wants to talk about baseball with me!)

Characters

TOMMY

TOMMY's our class clown. Sometimes he's really funny, but sometimes he is just annoying. Becca has a crush on him . . . but I'd never tell.

PETER

I think **PETER** is probably the smartest person I've ever met. Seriously. He's even smarter than our teachers! He's also one of my friends. Which is lucky, because sometimes he helps me with homework.

JENNY

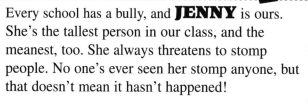

Every school has a bully, and **JENNY** is ours. She's the tallest person in our class, and the meanest, too. She always threatens to stomp people. No one's ever seen her stomp anyone, but that doesn't mean it hasn't happened!

ANNA

ANNA is the most popular girl at our school. Everyone wants to be friends with her. I think that's weird, because Anna can be really, really mean. I mostly try to stay away from her.

Cast of

CARLY is Anna's best friend. She always tries to act exactly like Anna does. She even wears the exact same clothes. She's never really been mean to me, but she's never been nice to me either!

CARLY

SYLVIA really wants to be best friends with Anna, but Anna isn't very nice to her. I'm not very close with Sylvia, but she's always pretty nice to me and my friends.

SYLVIA

BRAD

BRAD is our school's football star. He's also really, really cute. Becca and Monica know that I have a secret crush on him. I hope they never tell anyone!

Characters

NICK is my annoying seven-year-old neighbor. I get stuck babysitting him a lot. He likes to make me miserable. (Okay, he's not that bad ALL of the time . . . just most of the time.)

NICK

JIMMY

JIMMY is my big brother. I stay out of his way, and he stays out of mine. (But sometimes he does give me pretty good advice.)

UNCLE DIEGO is my dad's brother. He comes over a lot, usually to eat a meal with my family. I really like Uncle Diego. He's funny, and he treats me like an adult, not like a little kid.

UNCLE DIEGO

CHAPTER 1

THE MESS

"Ew! This is 𝒟𝒾𝒮𝒢𝒰𝒮𝒯𝒾𝒩𝒢!" **Monica** yelled.

She pulled a wad of chewed gum off one of the benches that lined the tree house walls. Then she brushed the dirt off the bench and sat down. She looked around.

"This is the messiest the tree house has ever been, Claudia," she said.

Every few months, Monica and **Becca** came over to help me clean up my tree house.

It wasn't like I was **bossing them around** — the tree house was where we usually hung out. So it was their mess too. We all worked together to get the tree house clean.

And Monica was right. **The tree house was a trash heap.**

Becca wrinkled her nose. "It smells like garbage in here," she said.

I held up a mushy brown apple core. "It's this," I said. "I told Nick to throw it outside for the birds. He **obviously** didn't."

Nick lived next door. **He was a seven-year-old temper tantrum on legs.** He never did what I told him, and he never picked up after himself.

"That's sick," Monica said. "Toss it outside into your compost bin."

"How did this mess get so *horrible* and 𝔻𝕀𝕊𝔾𝕌𝕊𝕋𝕀ℕ𝔾?" Becca asked. She set down a bucket of cleaning supplies. "I thought we always cleaned up after we hang out up here."

"We usually do. But we've been too busy lately," I said. "There hasn't been any time."

It was true. We had been busy. But **that was no excuse.** The tree house was our favorite place to go. We should have been keeping it clean, even if we were busy.

Ever since my big brother, **Jimmy**, decided he was too old for the tree house, it had been the place I went with my friends.

When we were little, we played with dolls and drew pictures in the tree house.

Now that we were teenagers, we **gossiped**, experimented with **makeup**, and **studied** in the tree house.

It was where I went to get away when I needed time alone or wanted to do a craft project. And unfortunately, it was where **Nick** went when he wanted to drive me nuts. That was most of the time.

"Let's sort through some of this stuff," I said. "We'll throw some of it away and keep some of it."

Monica picked up a dirty sock. I was pretty sure that it belonged to Nick. "Toss this or keep it?" she asked.

"Keep the 𝕊𝕄𝔼𝕃𝕃𝕐 sock," I said. "Nick won't care that it's gross."

"Let's divide everything up," Monica suggested. "That way we won't accidentally recycle Nick's sock."

Becca found a black marker in a big box of art supplies. She put Nick's sock in a grocery bag. Then she wrote KEEP on the bag.

She wrote COMPOST on another bag. I put the apple core inside.

Finally, Becca marked two more bags with the words RECYCLE and TRASH.

We filled the COMPOST bag with oak leaves, a peach pit, and another apple core. The RECYCLE bag got full **fast**, with homework papers, soda cans, and old magazines.

Before I could put all of our old magazines in the bag, Becca stopped me. "Let's look through this stack of magazines," she said. "We can use some of them for art projects."

Monica and I sat down next to her.

"So this is where I left it!" Monica said. She held up a copy of *Horse Newsletter*. That was her **favorite** magazine. "This issue has a list of must-have horse show gear. I wanted to keep it for when I get a horse. I thought it was gone!"

"We should clean the tree house more often," Becca joked. "We'd find all sorts of stuff we thought was **gone forever**!"

We sorted through the rest of the magazines. Most of them went into the RECYCLE bag, but **Becca** put a few of them into one of the storage benches. Then she **frowned**.

"What's this?" she asked, holding up a plastic bag. Then she squealed and dropped it. "There's **a dead thing** inside!" she yelled.

"That's Nick's **dried lizard**," I said. "He found it in Mom's garden." I put the lizard in the KEEP bag with Nick's sock.

Then I moved a pile of pillows. A gleam of color stuck between two pillows caught my eye. I blinked, looked closer, and gasped.

"What's wrong?" Becca asked.

"Is that my picture?" I whispered.

"You mean *THE picture*?" Monica asked.

Becca crossed her fingers. "Please, be Claudia's missing picture!" she said.

"Is it?" Monica asked.

I pulled it out. "**Yes**!" I yelled.

Becca exhaled with **relief**. "Thank goodness," she said, smiling.

I stared at the picture with a **goofy grin**.

The photo was one of my prized possessions. I had lost it, and I had been sure that I would **NEVER** see it again.

Becca had taken it six months ago.

One day, Principal Paul had sent us to the football field after school with a note for Coach Johnson.

Brad Turino had walked over to talk to Coach while we waited for Coach to read the note from Principal Paul.

The #1 Most Important Fact of My Life

I have a mad, secret crush on Brad Turino,

the best athlete, most gorgeous, nicest guy

in Pine Tree Middle School.

That day on the football field, Becca snapped a photo of Brad. In the picture, he was watching me the same way I watch him when he's not looking: with **adoring admiration**.

Of course, I was pretty sure Brad wasn't really watching me. It just looked like he was for that one split second.

I was **HEARTBROKEN** when I lost the picture. And Becca had deleted the file from her computer. We both felt *awful*.

"Please put that picture in a safe place this time," Becca told me.

"And have some copies made," Monica suggested.

"I will," I promised.

Monica and Becca left when the tree house was clean. I carefully carried my Brad picture back to the house.

As I was going inside, Jimmy bolted out the back door. **We almost collided.**

"Watch out!" I yelled.

Right away, I felt bad. I didn't mean to yell. I just didn't want my photo to get dirty or crumpled.

Jimmy wasn't annoyed, and he didn't snap at me. He was bursting with excitement. **"We're getting a swimming pool!"** he yelled.

CHAPTER 2

GOOD NEWS AND BAD NEWS

Jimmy doesn't make lists. If he did, teasing me would be #1 on his **Top Ten Most Fun Things To Do.** I knew better than to believe everything my brother said, so I was pretty sure he was lying about getting a pool.

"That's not 𝔽𝕌ℕℕ𝕐," I said.

"I wouldn't **joke** about getting a pool," Jimmy said. He looked annoyed. "Dad brought home the plans. Go inside and see for yourself."

He wasn't kidding. I whooped for joy and ran into the kitchen.

Mom was mixing biscuit batter. "You have **leaves in your hair**, Claudia," she told me.

"We cleaned the tree house," I said. Then I sat down at the counter. "Jimmy said we're getting a pool."

"That's right," Mom said.

"Fantastic!" I shouted. I giggled. I do that when **I'm so happy** it bubbles over. "So my friends and I can swim whenever we want?"

Mom nodded. "Yes, but —"

"I bet we'll have lots of company," I pointed out. "All our relatives will want to visit. And **old friends** you and Dad haven't seen in years."

Mom sighed. "Yes, but —"

I had a sudden, 𝓗𝓞𝓡𝓡𝓘𝓑𝓛𝓔 thought. I looked up sharply. "My bathing suit is faded and worn out!"

It was worn out, but it was also too little-kiddish. I didn't want a suit with little pink hearts on it anymore.

"Can I get a new one?" I pleaded. "Please, can I?"

Mom smiled. "Yes, but —"

"Thanks!" I said. I jumped up, grabbed my picture of Brad, and ran out. Monica and Becca would **flip** when I told them. I just had to decide how and when to break the news.

Method #1: The Blurt Out

Response: Squeals of surprise and delight.

Upside: A rush of super satisfaction.

Downside: The thrill is over too fast.

Method #2: Hint With Drawn-Out Suspense

Response: Worried demands to tell all.

Upside: Anticipation and total power.

Downside: Friends get mad before they get glad again.

Method #3: The Big Deal Event

Response: Excited pleas to tell; happy to wait.

Upside: Fun before and after the big, dramatic reveal!

Downside: None.

Method #3 was **the best**. If I didn't blab the instant Monica answered her phone.

Uncle Diego was watching TV in the living room. He came over for dinner a lot, so I figured he was just waiting to see if we were having **something good** that night.

"Hey, Claudia. Is your mom making dinner yet?" he asked.

"Yes, she's working on it," I said. "Have you seen Dad anywhere?"

"He's in the den with his pool plans," Uncle Diego said. "I'm really excited that you guys are getting a pool. **I can't wait!** Your house is going to be the place to be this summer."

"I know. I'm excited too," I told him. Then I hurried down the hall to my dad's den. The door was closed.

I paused for a second to calm down. My dad HATED it when people babbled.

I always babbled when I was:

A. Nervous

B. Scared

C. Excited

I was **really excited** about the pool!

I took a deep breath. Then I started to knock, but I totally lost my cool. Instead of knocking, I just 𝔹𝕌ℝ𝕊𝕋 through the door and threw my arms around Dad's neck.

"Thank you, thank you, thank you!" I yelled, hugging him. "I never thought we'd get a pool, not in a **million gazillion years**. I'm so happy I could **explode**!"

"I'd rather you didn't," Dad said.

Was he being **funny**? I wasn't sure. Dad almost never joked, and he wasn't smiling.

I forced myself to calm down. I stopped jumping and just jiggled with excitement.

"It's true, isn't it?" I asked. "We are **really** getting a pool?"

"Yes, it's true," Dad said. "I picked up the plans today. However —"

However = But = the bad part of something good.

What could be bad about getting a pool? I held my breath.

Dad sighed. Then he looked me in the eye and said, **"We have to cut down the tree-house-tree to make room for a swimming pool."**

CHAPTER 3

THE GOODBYE BEGINS

Dad's words hit hard.

Like Nick had **karate-kicked** me.

Like Jenny Pinski had STOMPED me.

Like all my friends had **dumped** me to become best friends with Anna Dunlap.

Only the hurt was **a thousand times worse.**

I didn't cry. Dad hated crying more than babbling. I excused myself and ran outside. Then **I burst into tears.**

"This can't be happening!" I wailed.

But it was happening, and I needed time for the **shock** to wear off.

An Unexplained Law of the Universe: Bad news takes longer than good news to sink in.

I did what I always did when I wanted to be alone.

I ran to the tree house.

But when I got to the tree-house-tree, I didn't climb the ladder. Sitting in the tree house wouldn't help this time.

The tree had to go so my family could have a pool. I had to get used to life without it.

Starting now.

I went to my room instead of going to the tree house. When I opened the door, I saw that Ping-ping was asleep on my pillow.

I sat on the end of the bed. Ping-ping opened one eye to make sure it was me. Then she went back to sleep.

I usually LOVED being in my room. It's where I kept my stuff. People were more important, but things reminded me about the reasons I loved my family and friends.

I had all the clothes, shoes, and furniture I needed because Mom and Dad took good care of me.

Grandma gave me the MP3 player. She knew Bad Dog was my **favorite** band. And she knew that Dad wouldn't let me play their CDs in the car.

My whole family chipped in to buy my computer at Dad's store. My brother set it up, and he fixed it when something went KABLOOEY.

That **proved** Jimmy loved me. Even though he wouldn't talk to me unless he absolutely had to.

Adam and I were Harmon County Hawks baseball fans. Adam gave me a team pennant for my birthday. It hung on the wall with an autographed picture of the players.

Uncle Diego asked everyone on the team to sign the picture when he worked at the stadium. Then he gave it to me for my birthday this year, when I turned thirteen.

Monica gave me a cat calendar every Christmas. I hung that next to the pencil portrait of Ping-ping that Becca drew.

Then I remembered Brad's picture. It was in the pocket of my jeans.

I had a special box that I kept in my closet. It's where I kept all the letters I got in the mail, birthday cards, and other special things.

That was the best place to keep Brad's picture. **It would be safe there.**

I put the photo in the box, and put the box back in my closet. My picture was safe, but the tree house wasn't. Just thinking about it made me *super sad* all over again.

Suddenly, music blasted from Jimmy's room across the hall. I jumped up to close my door.

"Claudia!" I heard Nick's voice. It sounded like he was in the living room. "Where are you?" he yelled. "Come on, I want to play."

I slammed the door and locked it. I did not want to deal with **my bratty neighbor**.

Ten seconds later, Nick pounded on my door. "Claudia! I want to go to the park. Are you in there?" he yelled.

"Come out or I'll put jelly in your backpack and squish it," Nick hollered.

My backpack was under my desk, so I wasn't worried.

Nick kicked the door. "Ow! I broke my toe!" he screamed.

I didn't say anything. Nick's stubbed toe was his own fault.

"Your mom wants you," Nick said. "She just made hot biscuits."

I knew he was trying to TRICK me, so I sat quietly.

Nick stopped yelling, but I could hear him breathing. He **huffed** and **puffed** when he was mad. Another minute passed. He kicked the door again and stomped down the hallway.

I waited another minute. I knew Nick wouldn't give up if he wanted something. He'd keep looking for me.

If I wanted to stay away from Nick, I had to **hide** where he wouldn't find me. There was only one place Nick wouldn't go.

I tiptoed down the hall. Then I paused at the top of the stairs and listened.

I heard my mom's voice downstairs. "I don't know where Claudia is, Nick," she said.

"She has to be somewhere," Nick insisted. "Kids don't just disappear unless —" He gasped. **"What if the Atomizer vaporized her?"** he asked, sounding worried. "He's Viper Man's arch enemy. He can vaporize somebody in three seconds."

"Hmm. Does the Atomizer live around here?" Mom asked.

"No," Nick said.

"Then I'm sure Claudia is fine," Mom said. "Check the **tree house**."

Nick ran outside. "Claudia!" he yelled. "Where are you?"

I ran down the stairs and ducked through the basement door. Nick wouldn't follow me into the basement.

He'd never admit it, but he was too scared  of the basement. I didn't blame him. It was too *creepy,* **dark, and damp** down there.

I hardly ever went down into the basement. Water dripped, pipes creaked, and spiders crawled on the walls. The windows were 𝔻𝕀ℝ𝕋𝕐, and very little sunlight shone in.

The basement was so creepy. It made me feel worse about the tree house.

I had to get out of my bad mood.

Only one thing might lift my spirits.

After I was pretty sure Nick was gone, I crept back upstairs and dialed the phone.

"Hi, Monica," I said. "Call everyone and meet me at the Pizza Palace. **Right away.**"

CHAPTER 4

WHAT POOL PROBLEM?

The Pizza Palace was crowded. Anna and
Carly were walking out just as I started to walk in.

Anna wrinkled her nose like *she smelled something
putrid*. That's my grandma's word for something that
smells gross, like stinking rot.

"Is something living in your hair?"
Anna asked.

Oh no! **A spider?**

I ran my fingers through my hair. Anna laughed.
Then I realized she was being mean.

"Your hair looks like a **bird's nest**, Claudia,"
Carly said.

OOPS. I had rushed out of the house without
washing up or changing clothes. And I was in the
basement and the dirty tree house!

I didn't want to bother to explain my **messy**
appearance. So I didn't try.

"Gotta go," I said. Then I walked inside.

I heard Anna stamp her foot and then stomp  off. I smiled. It wasn't **fun** to zing someone who didn't care.

Inside, I spotted my friends sitting in a corner booth. Adam stood up, and I slid in beside Monica.

"We already ordered," Peter said.

"Sodas for everyone," Becca added.

"And an extra-large pepperoni-pineapple pizza," Tommy said.

I loved pineapple in fruit salad. I hated it on pizza. Everybody knew that, but I was too upset to complain.

"Topped with red hot peppers, black olives, and fish slivers," Tommy continued. "I call it the **so-gross-nobody-else-will-eat-it anchovy special**."

"Oh," I said.

Everybody stared at me.

"What's wrong?" Monica asked.

"It must be serious," **Adam** said. "Claudia usually GAGS just thinking about pineapple-anchovy pizza."

"No pineapple and no **salty little fish**," **Peter** said. "Just pepperoni. Honest."

"Okay," I said. I sighed.

"You're a **mess**," Adam said, noticing my hair and my dirty clothes. "Did you dive for home plate or get in a fight?"

"No and no," I replied. Then I said, "I'm getting an in-ground swimming pool with a diving board and water slide."

The So-Surprised-I-Don't-Believe-It Chain Reaction

1. Blink: Did I hear that right?

2. Stare: She really said it!

3. Frown: Is this a joke?

"Are you kidding?" Adam asked.

"No, we're really getting a pool," I said. I sighed again. "But we have to cut down the **tree-house-tree** to make room."

"So what?" Tommy exclaimed. **"Teenagers do not hang out in tree houses."**

"Pool parties at your house will be awesome," Becca said. "Right?"

I nodded. "Yes, but —"

"Yay," Becca said. "**I can't wait.** You can invite the whole school!"

"Anna never invites us to her pool parties," Monica said. "Never."

"Not even once," Becca added. "You shouldn't invite her to yours."

"Anna wouldn't come to a party at Claudia's house anyway," Peter pointed out.

That was probably true.

Anna was:

1. Pretty

2. Popular

3. Particular.

She only did cool stuff that was:

1. Expensive

2. Exclusive

3. Extraordinary.

"Then we'll have to make Anna SORRY she missed Claudia's first pool party," Monica said.

"How?" Tommy asked. Then he blew his straw wrapper at Adam.

"Easy," Becca said. "If everyone raves about it, Anna will be jealous."

"I don't care about Anna. I can't wait to play Keep Away and Marco Polo," Adam said. Then he wadded up Tommy's straw wrapper and threw it back.

Tommy ducked. The wrapper flew into the booth behind him and hit someone's head.

It was Sylvia. She slowly turned around. **"Who did that?"** she asked.

Everyone in our booth pointed to someone else.

Sylvia **giggled** and turned back around.

"I have to buy a new bathing suit!" Becca exclaimed.

"I need a new one too," Monica said. "Let's go to the mall tomorrow."

My friends were **so excited** I had no choice. **I had to pick the pool over the tree.** But there was one bright side.

Anna's pool was the one place everyone in the seventh grade wanted to hang out.

That was going to change.

CHAPTER 5

NIGHTMARE

Bad dreams gave me the shivers. **Really bad dreams** made me sick.

Dreaming about the tree-house-tree was like being trapped in a horror movie. It made me feel worse than sick. **It made me feel horrible.**

The Murdered Oak Nightmare

NIGHT - CORTEZ BACKYARD

There's a full moon. The tree-house OAK TREE looks like a spooky skeleton. CLAUDIA is wearing a nightgown. She looks up at the tree.

CLAUDIA (sadly): I'm sorry, Tree. My family and friends want a swimming pool. We have to cut you down.

OAK TREE (begging): **I'm your friend too!** Please, don't cut me down.

CLAUDIA: Sorry, Tree. We took a vote. You lost.
Goodbye.

An Oak Tree branch grabs Claudia's nightgown.
She S̲C̲R̲E̲A̲M̲S̲ but she can't break free.

OAK TREE (creepy wail): **I don't want to die!**

That's when I woke up.

Shaking.

With a stomach ache.

And cold chills.

The tree nightmare was the worst nightmare I'd
ever had. **It felt real**, except for the tree talking and
grabbing me.

After a nightmare, I usually fell back asleep. And I
usually didn't remember my dreams in the morning.

This time I couldn't sleep, and I didn't forget. I sat
in bed wide awake.

It was just before sunrise. **Dim light and shadows =
gloomy room = doom and gloom thoughts.**

I felt guilty about cutting down the tree. The big oak was like an old friend.

Oak Tree Memories

1. Spotting tiny green leaf buds in spring.
2. Mom pushing me on the swing.
3. Jumping in piles of fall leaves.
4. Helping Dad string Christmas lights.
5. Handing Dad nails when he built the tree house.

The tree was an important part of my childhood.

Cutting down the tree = stop being a kid.

I was thirteen. I couldn't cling to kid stuff forever. But the tree wasn't just for kids. It was good for a thirteen-year-old, too.

1. Swinging helps me think when I'm stumped.
2. Being in the tree house keeps Nick busy.
3. Total privacy for talking with my friends.

How could I even think about cutting down the tree?

Bright morning sunlight came in my window. It chased away the gloom and cleared my head.

If I wanted to keep the tree, my friends would understand.

Wouldn't they?

CHAPTER 6

ANNA AMBUSH

Monica's mom drove us to the mall the next day after school. I didn't talk about **my keep-the-tree-or-get-a-pool problem.** I had to wait for the right moment.

I wanted my friends to change their minds. But I didn't want them to feel guilty about cutting down the old oak.

Guilt felt like being:

1. Sucked into a stinky swamp.

2. Swarmed by a million beetles.

3. Stuck in a deep dark pit.

"Where should we go first?" Monica asked.

"Let's go to Music Central and listen to music," Becca suggested.

We spent ten minutes listening to music. Monica bought a CD. "We can listen to it in the tree house sometime," she said.

The **right moment** had arrived.

"Maybe not," I said.

"Is your CD player broken?" Monica asked.

"No," I said. "We won't have a place to meet."

"That's right!" Monica exclaimed. **"Bye—bye tree house, hello pool!"**

"We'll find another meeting place," Becca said.

"Maybe one that's better," Monica added.

My **no-guilt plan** had backfired. Becca and Monica wouldn't miss the tree house. They wanted a pool more.

"Let's go to **Flare**," Becca suggested. "We can start looking for bathing suits."

Flare was the most popular store in the mall. They had the cutest clothes and the best sales. And they played cool music.

We walked up and down the aisles looking at everything. My mom called that **browsing**. I called it **teenage torment**. I didn't have enough money to buy everything I wanted.

Even though I could spend money I earned however I felt like it, I didn't want to blow it on clothes. I was saving up to buy a car **the day I turned 16!**

"I love this!" Monica said. She pulled a blue top off a rack. It had long sleeves and pink flowers on the bottom.

"That would look GREAT with jeans," Becca said.

"Look at this bag!" I exclaimed, lifting it off the shelf. The bag was bright red. Red was my favorite color. I looked inside the bag. "It's even got a cell phone pocket," I told my friends.

"You don't have a cell phone," Monica reminded me.

A cell phone of my own was #1 on my **wish list.** But Dad said I couldn't get one until I was 15. I put the red bag back.

Becca held up a fuzzy purple sweater. It had **feathery purple fringe** and orange pom-poms on the neckline. "This is the *ugliest* sweater I've ever seen," she said.

"Who would wear that?" I asked.

"Someone who wants to look like a **plucked purple chicken**," Monica joked.

We laughed all the way to the swimsuit racks.

"Two-piece or one?" Becca asked.

"A one-piece is better for water games," I said.

"But a two-piece is better for getting a **suntan**," Becca said.

"These are so **cute**!" Monica said. She picked out a blue suit with a seashell design.

Becca chose a flower-print bikini with a matching beach top.

I found a crimson red suit. A **white and silvery bubble pattern** curved across the front. I held it up for Monica and Becca to see.

"Do you like this one?" I asked.

Monica nodded. "It's the PERFECT color for you," she told me.

Just then, Anna and Carly walked up to us.

"That suit is too fancy for the lake," Anna said. "*Fish love to nibble sparkly things.*"

Munched for lunch by fish! The idea made my skin crawl.

"And the water in the Community Center pool will ruin it," Carly said. "They use too much chlorine."

"That's why your hair turns **green** and feels like **straw** after you swim there," Anna said.

Becca smiled. "Actually, Claudia won't be wearing her new suit in the Community Center pool," she told Anna.

"Or the lake," Monica added.

"Well, if she's not wearing it at the Community Center or the lake, where's she going to wear it?" Carly asked, looking at the three of us.

Monica smiled. "She needs it for the **new pool** in her back yard," she said.

"Did you get a new kiddie pool, Claudia?" Anna cooed in **baby talk.**

I rolled my eyes. I hated being the target of Anna's sharp tongue.

Teasing made me feel:

1. **Hurt when the tease was mean.**

2. **Embarrassed when the tease was true.**

3. **Mad when the tease was unfair.**

I almost never thought of a snappy comeback fast enough. So Anna usually got away with being a jerk. This time I **fought back** with facts.

"Actually," I said, "I'm getting a Swimmer's Cove deluxe in-ground pool."

"With a diving board and water slide," Monica added.

Becca giggled.

Carly's mouth fell open.

"No, you're not," **Anna** said.

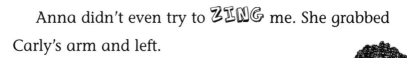

"Yes, she is," Monica said.

I nodded and smiled.

Anna didn't even try to ZING me. She grabbed Carly's arm and left.

"Did you see Anna's face?" Becca asked.

Monica laughed. "Total shock," she said.

I didn't get the best of Anna very often. It felt good. But now she knew about the pool. So I had to get one, or suffer the horrible consequences.

Anna would never let me forget it if I said I was getting a pool and then didn't. It would hang over my head like a permanent black cloud.

Every day until our high school graduation, she would remind everyone about the time I said I was getting a pool but didn't.

I couldn't take that risk. Anna was bad enough. **Anna with a reason to tease was awful.**

I had to grow up sooner or later. It might as well be now.

Tommy was right.

Tree houses were for kids. Teenagers needed pools.

CHAPTER 7

IT'S ALIVE!

Nick had **bad *mood radar***. He knew when I was cranky or worried or upset. Then he was like a big zit on the end of my nose. A horror that wouldn't go away!

"What are you doing?" Nick asked. He stared down at me, holding a glass of lemonade in one hand.

"Sunbathing," I said.

"Why?" Nick asked.

"To get a tan," I said.

"Why?" Nick asked again.

I was tanning because my new suit had smaller straps than my old suit. The tan lines looked **weird**. I needed to fix my tan.

Nick didn't want to know that. **He just wanted to drive me crazy.**

"Because," I answered.

Something wet fell on my leg. I sat up with a gasp.

There was a drop of water on my leg.

"Did you SPIT on me?" I demanded.

"No," Nick said. He showed me the ice cube melting in his hand. He ate it. Then he took another cube out of his lemonade. "I won't drip on you again," he told me. "I'll drool on you next time."

Unexplained Law of The Universe: Little kids think disgusting stuff is funny.

I rolled onto my stomach so I could watch him. I **didn't dare close my eyes.**

"It's **too hot** out here," Nick said.

"Go back inside," I suggested.

As usual, Nick didn't do what I told him. He sat in the shade of the tree-house-tree.

"When are you getting the pool?" Nick asked.

"Soon," I said.

"Are they going to dig a big hole?" Nick asked.

"Yep," I said. "Right where you're sitting."

Nick frowned. It wasn't his **mad frown**. He was puzzled. "Wait. What about the tree-house-tree?" he asked.

"They have to cut it down to make room for the pool," I explained.

Nick gasped with **a little squeak**. "What do you mean?" he asked.

I'd never heard him gasp before. Nothing ever shocked Nick.

Until now.

"You can't cut down the tree!" Nick wailed. **"It's alive!"**

I didn't want to think about that. My choice wasn't just between the tree and the pool anymore. It was way more complicated.

Anna knew. If we didn't get a pool, Anna would tell everyone that **I lied to look cool**. Even though that wasn't true at all.

"Everybody wants a pool, Nick," I told him. "We all decided."

"Not me!" Nick yelled. **He burst into tears.**

I was shocked. Nick cared about the tree! I tried to make him feel better.

"You'll have more fun in a pool," I said.

"Can I splash you?" Nick asked. He sniffled.

"Yes," I said, "but only if I'm already wet."

"I don't believe you," Nick said.

"Why not?" I said. "I never lie to you."

"Yes, you do," Nick said. "One time, you promised we could sleep out in the tree house for the whole night. **You promised.** We never did, and now it's too late. The tree house is getting cut down. We can't sleep in it. **So that was a lie.**"

Breaking a promise was as bad as lying. I couldn't go back on my word.

"It's not too late!" I exclaimed. "We can sleep out tonight."

Right away, I wished I hadn't said that.

Sleep Out Checklist

1. sleeping bags
2. flashlights
3. scary book
4. bottled water
5. snacks

Nick complaint #1: There's no TV!

Solution: Explain why, even if it doesn't help.

"Pioneers didn't have TV," I said. "Or computers or video games or radio."

"No way!" Nick exclaimed. "What did they do all night?"

"They went to bed after dinner," I said.

"I'm not tired!" Nick yelled, scowling.

"Good," I said. "We've got work to do." Then Nick and I climbed the ladder.

"I'll put everything on this bench," I told Nick. "That way we can find things in the dark."

Nick complaint #2: I hate the dark!

Solution: Let him keep his flashlight on.

"Isn't this exciting?" I asked as I unrolled the sleeping bags.

"No," Nick told me. He aimed his flashlight in my face.

"Lighten up!" I teased. "We'll have fun."

"I won't," Nick said. He stuck out his lower lip. Sometimes nothing made him happy.

Nick Complaint #3: I'm hungry

Solution: Give him an apple.

I unpacked our supplies while Nick ate.

Nick ate half the apple. Then he opened a bench.

"Do not put the apple core in there," I said.
"Last time you did that you left it there and it
stunk up the whole tree house. Just put it down."

"But it's garbage!" Nick said. "It's going to get mushy
and smelly."

**Unexplained Law of the Universe: Little kids don't like
to touch disgusting stuff they think is funny.**

"Throw it outside," I said. "You can put it in
the compost in the morning."

Nick Complaint #4: I'm bored.
Solution: Read a ghost story.

"I brought a book," I said. I held up my new copy of
Phantom High, The Revenge of Eerie Eileen.

Nick complaint #5: That book doesn't have pictures.

Solution: Just read the scary parts.

"Imagine the pictures in your head," I explained.

"Is Viper Man in it?" Nick asked.

VIPERMAN

"No," I said. "Just lie down and listen." I began reading in a low spooky voice.

Nick was asleep when I reached the end of Chapter One. I closed the book, closed my eyes, and nodded off.

I jerked awake when Nick screamed.

Nick complaint #6: I'm scared!

Solution: Stop shaking, turn on flashlight, and act brave.

It was really, really dark. The batteries in Nick's flashlight were dead.

"It's okay," I said. I gave him my flashlight. "I'm right here. Did you have a bad dream?"

"No," **Nick** said. "All the creepy noises woke me up."

I stopped talking and listened. I heard creaks and groans.

Unexplained Law of the Universe: Sounds are louder at night.

"It's not anything. It's just creaky boards and tree branches," I said.

"The tree's trying to tell you something, Claudia," Nick whispered. "It doesn't want to die. You can't let them kill it!"

"Don't be silly," I said. I read another chapter of the book. Finally, Nick went back to sleep.

I didn't.

I wanted to keep the tree and get a pool, but I couldn't have both.

I had to choose and stick to my decision.

Once the tree was gone, **I wouldn't be able to change my mind.**

CHAPTER 8

MEETING PLACE TRYOUTS

"We **can't** hang out at the tree house. Some people are coming to see what they'll need to cut it down. And we **can't** hang out in my room," I told Becca and Monica the next day after school.

All week, we'd been planning on getting together to try different hairstyles, do our nails, and go through fashion magazines to pick out dream wardrobes. **And Becca was going to dye my hair.** We were supposed to meet at my house.

"What's wrong with your room?" Monica asked.

"Nick and Jimmy are both at my house," I said.

"Then we **REALLY** don't want to be there," Becca agreed.

We would be trying to **look beautiful.** Nick made us feel like **bozos.**

Last time, he yelled, "Look at the clowns!" and rolled around on the floor, laughing.

"Jimmy is worse," Monica said.

My brother would pound on the door. Then he'd throw it open and **roar like a monster**.

He thought it was funny to scare us. Believe me, smearing lipstick and mascara wasn't funny. That stuff was hard to get off!

We decided to meet at Monica's house.

Becca and I brought our supplies in backpacks. We listened to music while we unpacked in Monica's room.

When everything was set out, Becca looked at me. "Ready, Claudia?" she asked.

Becca wanted to put red highlights in my hair. I was pretty sure **my parents would hate it.** I thought it would look **awesome**. If it didn't, my hair would grow out.

"I'm ready as I'll ever be," I said. I sat in Monica's desk chair and closed my eyes.

Becca started to brush my hair. Just then, the bedroom door banged open.

Monica's step-sister ran in. "I want to play!"
Angela shrieked.

"We're not **playing**," Monica said as she put on
blue eyeshadow. "We're doing makeup."

"I want makeup!" Angela yelled. Just like Nick, she
never spoke softly. She 𝔸𝕃𝕎𝔸𝕐𝕊 yelled.

"You're only eight," Becca said.
"That's too young."

"No, it's not!" Angela yelled. She jumped up and
down. "I like blue eyes. And I want curly hair like
Claudia. Please, please, please!"

We all looked at each other.

Getting rid of Nick on makeup day was easy.
We just **threatened** to paint his nails. Or curl his
eyelashes. Or style his hair with gobs of gel that
smells like flowers.

The only way to get rid of Angela was to paint
her nails, curl her eyelashes, and style her hair. **We
gave in.**

"Me first. I'll sit still," Angela said.

She pushed me off the desk chair and sat down. "I want glitter," she told us.

Becca picked out pink lipstick. Angela wanted **red lipstick.**

I suggested ponytails. Angela wanted *braids.*

Monica held up a bottle of red nail polish. Angela wanted **blue.**

When we finished, Angela look like a **Junior Miss Beauty Pageant Princess.** And it was time for Becca and me to go home.

Monica's room rating: Snacks = + 5

Sister = - 5

Total = 0

* * *

The next day, Monica, Becca, and I met in the park. Usually, we only hung out at the tree house, unless we were watching something on TV or going to the mall. But sometimes we could hang out other places too.

Becca made a list, and we discussed our options.

"What about Roaring Rock?" Becca asked.

"It's in the park," I said.

"Which is GREAT for exercise or playing games," Monica pointed out.

"But **not** for arts and crafts or make-up," I said. "Or when it's raining."

Roaring Rock rating: **Outside activities = + 5**

                                Inside activities = − 5

                                Total = 0

Becca read #2 on her list. "The back booth at Pizza Palace," she said.

"We'll have snacks and drinks," I said.

"But **no privacy**," Monica said.

"Good point." Becca frowned. "Someone might hear our **secrets**."

"That could be a disaster!" I said. We would be **totally mortified** if anyone heard us!

Pizza Palace rating: Snacks & drinks = + 5

No privacy = − 5

Total = 0

"What's our third choice?" I asked Becca.

"My house," Becca said.

"I don't know," Monica said. **"Your mom is always bugging us."**

Becca's mother wasn't nosy. And she didn't think we were doing something wrong. She was just too nice!

She brought snacks. Then she brought drinks. She was interested in our projects and liked to help. But we didn't want a **mom** hanging out with us all the time.

"I didn't mean my room," Becca said. "We can use the garden shed."

Becca's garden shed stood in a corner of her back yard. There were two windows and a door on the front.

The shed was white with red shutters, just like Becca's house. There was even a little rose bush planted right next to the door.

"It's **really cute**," I said.

"It's just like a tree house on the ground," Monica said. "PERFECT!"

We thought we'd found the perfect place. But then we looked inside.

The shed wasn't like the tree house at all. Not even one tiny bit.

The tree house had open windows that let in sunlight and fresh air. The small shed windows were covered with grime. There was dirt on the floor and cobwebs in the corners. A *gross*, **musty smell** stung my nose.

The tree house had built-in benches where we could sit and store our stuff.

The shed was full of old tools, pots, and bags of soil. Becca's dad stored the lawnmower on one side. The shelves on the other side were loaded with boxes and rusty cans.

Becca looked **disappointed**. "I'm sorry, you guys. I didn't know the shed was so **dark** and *gloomy*," she admitted.

"It's okay. It will look better after we clean it up," Monica said.

"And we'll have **privacy** here," I said.

Becca smiled. "Then let's get to work," she said.

I picked up a moldy rag and reached for a broom. Monica squealed, and **a mouse** ran for cover. A dust cloud made Becca sneeze.

We sorted, swept, and cleaned for two hours.

When we finished, half the floor was clear. The cobwebs were gone, and the windows were clean. But the walls still smelled like old leaves, and very little light came in.

The shed was almost as **dreary** as my basement.

Garden Shed rating: No light = – 5

Junk = – 5

Privacy = + 5

Last option = +10

Total = + 5

We didn't have a choice anymore. After next Saturday, the shed would be the only meeting place we had.

CHAPTER 9

PROS AND CONS

Adam had a baseball game Friday afternoon. I sat with our friends to cheer on his team. The Panthers won 4 to 3. After the game, Adam walked over to us.

"Great game!" Tommy said. He stood up and gave Adam a **high five.**

"Have a seat, Adam," I said. I scooted over to make room on the bleachers.

"Have some water," Peter said. He gave Adam a bottle of water.

"Thanks," Adam said. He took a long swallow. Then he wiped sweat off his face and said, "Too bad your pool isn't ready, Claudia. I could REALLY use a cool dip."

"Me too!" Becca said, fanning herself with a folded paper. "It's sizzling hot."

"I'm counting the days," Monica said. "Just don't throw me in."

"Pool party pooper," Tommy said. "It's no fun if we can't push people in."

"No way!" Peter said. He looked **horrified.**

"It's just water," Tommy said. "Not bog mud or lake goo."

"I don't swim very well," Peter explained. "Once at the lake Anna said I swim like a waddling walrus."

"I'll help you," Monica offered. "You'll learn fast when we can practice all the time."

"Good point," Peter said, smiling. "And I won't feel so **self-conscious** in Claudia's pool. You guys won't tease me."

"No teasing. The point is to have fun," Tommy said. "Knock-knock."

"Who's there?" Becca asked.

"Splash," Tommy said.

Becca played along. "Splash who?"

"Splash you!" Tommy yelled. He flicked bottled water at Becca.

Becca giggled and ducked. "I can't wait to have water fights in Claudia's pool!" she said.

I smiled, but I wasn't as happy as my friends. I walked home with a heavy heart.

"How was the game?" Mom asked when I walked into the kitchen.

"Adam's team WON," I told her. I sat at the kitchen counter.

"Great," Mom said.

Mom always gave me good advice when I had a problem. I had a really big problem now.

"If there are good reasons for two choices, how do you decide?" I asked.

"Make a list of pros and cons," Mom said. "Write down the good and bad things about each choice. That will help you think about your reasons."

"That's a **great idea**!" I said. I jumped off the stool and ran upstairs. I sat at my desk with a pen and a piece of paper.

Pros for getting a pool:

1. A pool is cool, period.

2. No more wishing for invites to Anna's pool.

3. Adam can swim laps.

4. Peter can learn to swim without being teased.

5. Becca and Tommy will have a good excuse to hang out.

FYI: I knew Becca liked Tommy, and I was pretty sure that Tommy liked Becca, too.

Cons for getting a pool:

1. I'll have to watch Nick, even when my friends are over.

2. Everyone will want to hang out at my house all the time, and I'll have to clean up.

3. We have to cut down the tree-house-tree.

Pros for keeping the tree:

1. The tree is alive.

2. I love the tree and the tree house.

Cons for keeping the tree:

1. Jimmy will be mad at me forever if we don't get a pool.

2. My friends will be disappointed if we don't get a pool.

3. Anna and her friends will laugh and point and call me a lying loser every time they see me until twelfth grade if I don't get a pool.

4. It would be really fun to have a pool.

There were more good reasons to get the pool. But I'd still feel guilty about cutting down the tree. It was at least fifty years old. Maybe a hundred!

I couldn't decide.

Then the phone rang.

I picked up. "Hello?"

"Hi, Claudia! This is Brad."

I almost fell over. My cheeks got warm and my stomach did flip-flops. **Brad Turino was calling me!**

Then I choked up.

I stumbled over my words whenever I talk to Brad in person. But at least in person, I could smile and nod to cover it up. He couldn't see me on the phone! **I had to say something.**

"Hi, B-B-Brad," I stammered. "Uh—what's up?"

"I'm just calling to say hi," Brad said.

"Oh," I said. I giggled. "Hi."

"I heard you're getting a pool," Brad said. "That is so cool. Swimming at **Anna's** house isn't much fun. She's got too many silly rules.'

"What kind of rules?" I asked. The words rolled off my tongue with no trouble!

"**Stupid stuff,**" Brad said. "No swimming laps, no water games that splash, no cannonballs."

"That's no fun!" I exclaimed. **Wow!** Talking to Brad on the phone was easy.

Brad laughed. "I hope you'll invite me over sometime. I love swimming!"

"You can come over any time you want," I said.

Swimming pool = Brad Turino

That was the best reason of all.

The pool won.

CHAPTER 10

FOND FAREWELL

I wanted Brad to visit my house more than anything.

Almost.

When I woke up Saturday morning, I realized I wanted to save the tree more.

It was the big day. I didn't want breakfast. I couldn't eat when I was *miserable*. I sipped O.J. and tried to look happy.

"What's wrong, Claudia?" Mom asked.

"Nothing," I told her. Then I sighed. "I'm just tired."

I didn't want to make my family feel bad. Everybody else wanted the pool.

"Too excited to sleep?" Dad asked as he walked in. He put the pool plans on the counter.

"Sort of," I said. I had been too upset to sleep.

"I'm going to the store," Dad told Mom.
"I'll be back before the tree service gets here."

My stomach tightened. My throat went dry. **Tears** welled up in my eyes. I blinked them back.

Dad left and Mom went into the laundry room.

I grabbed the plans and ran outside. I had to do something. I didn't have a plan to save the tree. I hoped something would come to me.

I stopped under the tree and looked up. The leafy branches were like a huge green umbrella. The day was already hot, but the shade was cool.

I didn't care if there were more good reasons to get a pool. There was one gigantic reason to keep the tree.

The tree was a living member of the **family**.

And the old oak didn't know it was doomed.

I had to do something!

Suddenly, I was inspired.

They wouldn't cut down the tree if I was in it!

I scrambled up the ladder.

I set the pool plans on a bench and stared out the window. I knew my idea wouldn't work. **Dad could make me come down.** But trying something silly was better than doing nothing.

I watched Ping-ping chase a butterfly across the yard. It was a big yard. A really big yard.

Then an idea struck me. Why did the new pool have to go in that spot? There was lots of room in the yard.

Good question!

I unrolled the pool plans. I looked out the window. Then I looked back at the plans.

Outside, Ping-ping ran through my mom's garden.

Then inspiration struck again. **BAM**! Like a bolt of lightning.

There was almost as much room on the other side of the yard, where my mom's garden was! If she'd agree to move the garden, we could **have a pool and keep the tree!**

I grabbed the plans and ran toward the house.

Nobody would care if the pool was a little shorter. And Mom wouldn't mind losing her garden. I'd help her plant more flowers. They grow fast.

But we couldn't grow another tree-house-tree.

CHAPTER 11

P.S.

My family was **thrilled** with my idea. They didn't care that the pool would be smaller, and no one thought it was 𝒞𝐻𝐼𝐿𝐷𝐼𝒮𝐻 to want to keep the old oak. Not even Jimmy.

Funny thing: Nobody in my family wanted to cut down the tree-house-tree. But everyone thought everyone else wanted a pool more. So nobody spoke up to save the tree. **They were all glad I did.**

I helped Mom plant a new garden in front of our house. **It looked great!**

Nick was so happy he didn't throw a tantrum for a week! He and I sat in the tree house to watch the machines dig the hole for the pool. He loved it.

The day we filled the pool, I invited all of my friends over to swim in it.

Including Brad Turino.

About the Author

Diana G. Gallagher lives in Florida with her husband and five dogs, four cats, and a cranky parrot. Her hobbies are gardening, garage sales, and grandchildren. She has been an English equitation instructor, a professional folk musician, and an artist. However, she had aspirations to be a professional writer at the age of twelve. She has written dozens of books for kids and young adults.

About the Illustrator

Brann Garvey lives in Minneapolis, Minnesota with his wife, Keegan, their dog, Lola, and their very fat cat, Iggy. Brann graduated from Iowa State University with a bachelor of fine arts degree. He later attended the Minneapolis College of Art and Design, where he studied illustration. In his free time, Brann enjoys being with his family and friends. He brings his sketchbook everywhere he goes.

Glossary

admiration (ad-mur-AY-shuhn)—respect

appearance (uh-PEER-uhnss)—the way something looks

backfired (BAK-fye-urd)—did not work out as planned

chlorine (KLOR-een)—a gas with a strong smell that is added to water to kill harmful germs

collided (kuh-LIDE-id)—crashed together forcefully

compost (KOM-pohst)—a mixture of rotted leaves, vegetables, manure, etc., that is added to soil to make it richer

dreary (DREER-ee)—dull and miserable

exclusive (ek-SKLOO-siv)—if something is exclusive, only certain people are allowed to know about or do it

particular (pur-TIK-yuh-lur)—if someone is particular, they are careful about details and prefer things to be done a certain way

privacy (PRYE-vuh-see)—being away from other people, where you can't be seen or heard

torment (TOR-ment)—great pain or suffering

Discussion Questions

1. What would you do if, like Claudia, you had to choose between the tree house and the new pool? Explain your answer.

2. Tommy says that pools are for teenagers and tree houses are for kids. But Claudia thinks both things are for teenagers. What are some other things that people might think are for kids, but you know that teenagers like too?

3. Claudia figures out a solution to her pool problem. What do you think would have happened if the tree had been cut down? What would have happened if the pool hadn't been built? Talk about the different possibilities.

Writing Prompts

1. Claudia lists many reasons she likes her tree house. Where is your favorite place to hang out? Make a list of reasons why you like to be there.

2. Claudia spends most of her time with her friends Becca and Monica. Write about your closest friend. What is that person like? What do you like to do together?

3. Design your perfect back yard. What does it contain? Don't forget to include things that other people in your family might like.

MORE FUN
with Claudia!

THE COMPLICATED LIFE OF
Claudia
Cristina
Cortez
BY DIANA G. GALLAGHER

HIRED OR FIRED?

REALISTIC FICTION

BAD LUCK BRIDESMAID

THE COMPLICATED LIFE OF
Claudia Cristina Cortez
BY DIANA G. GALLAGHER

BEWARE!

THE COMPLICATED LIFE OF
Claudia Cristina Cortez
BY DIANA G. GALLAGHER

SOLD!

THE COMPLICATED LIFE OF
Claudia Cristina Cortez
BY DIANA G. GALLAGHER

Claudia Cristina Cortez

Just like every other thirteen-year-old girl, Claudia Cristina Cortez has a complicated life. Whether she's studying for the big Quiz Show, babysitting her neighbor, Nick, avoiding mean Jenny Pinski, planning the seventh-grade dance, or trying desperately to pass the swimming test at camp, Claudia goes through her complicated life with confidence, cleverness, and a serious dash of cool.

David Mortimore Baxter

David is a great kid, but he has one big problem — he can't stop talking. These wildly humorous stories, told by David himself, will show readers just how much trouble a boy and his mouth can get into, whether he's going on a class trip, trying to find a missing neighbor, running a detective agency, or getting lost in the wild. David is amiable, engaging, cool, and smart enough to realize that growing up is the biggest adventure of all.

with David!

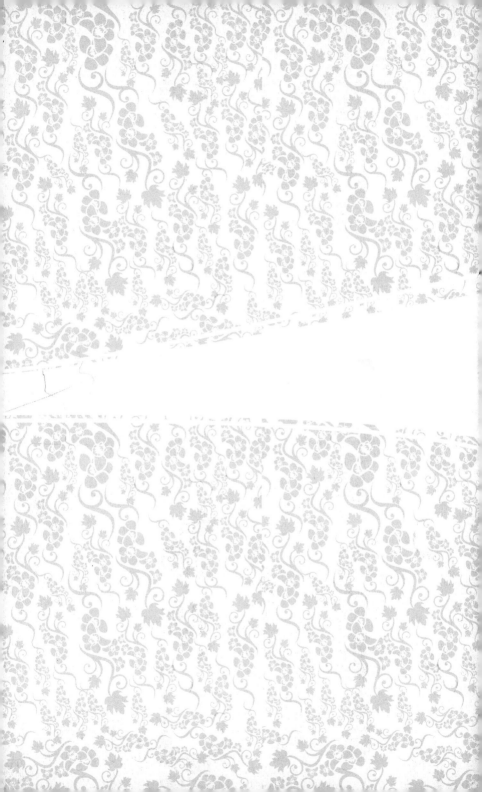